To Marie Wabbes

First U.S. edition published 1992
by Thomasson-Grant, Inc.
Copyright ©1990 Editions Dessain, Liège.
Original title: *Trois chats*. First published in
1990 by Editions Dessain, Belgium.
This book, or any portions thereof, may not
be reproduced in any form without written
permission from the publisher.
Printed in Belgium.

99 98 97 96 95 94 93 92 5 4 3 2 1

Any inquiries should be directed to
Thomasson-Grant, Inc.
One Morton Drive, Suite 500
Charlottesville, VA 22901
804-977-1780

Library of Congress
Cataloging-in-Publication Data

Brouillard, Anne.
        [Trois chats. English]
    Three cats /Anne Brouillard.
            p.   cm.
        Translation of: Trois chats.
        Summary: Three cats leap from a branch
into water and exchange places with three fish who
are splashed up onto the branch.
        ISBN 0-934738-97-1
        [1. Cats—Fiction. 2. Fishes—Fiction.
3. Stories without words.]   I. Title.
PZ7.B79975Th 1992
[E]—dc20   91-34180
                                          CIP
                                          AC

Thomasson-Grant

Anne Brouillard

THREE CATS

Thomasson-Grant
Charlottesville, Virginia